Skinny and **Fats,**
Best Friends

by Cari Meister

illustrated by

Steve Björkman

Holiday House / New York

For Marni, the skinny one
—C. M.

For Diane, Marsha, Debbie, and Jean,
gym buddies through thick and thin
—S. B.

Reading Level: 2.3

Text copyright © 2002 by Cari Meister
Illustrations copyright © 2002 by Steve Björkman
All Rights Reserved
Printed in the United States of America
www.holidayhouse.com
First Edition

Library of Congress Cataloging-in-Publication Data

Meister, Cari.
Skinny and Fats, best friends / by Cari Meister;
illustrated by Steve Björkman.
p.   cm.
Summary: Two best friends, Skinny the rabbit and Fats the pig,
share adventures when they build a rocket and bake some pies.
ISBN 0-8234-1692-5 2865 2815 19/02
[1. Best friends—Fiction. 2. Friendship—Fiction.
3. Rabbits—Fiction. 4. Pigs—Fiction.]
I. Björkman, Steve, ill. II. Title.

PZ7.M515916 Sk 2002
[E]—dc21   2001051534

Contents

Chapter One
Best Friends

"Skinny?" said Fats.

"Yes, Fats?" said Skinny.

"You are my best friend," said Fats.

"That is right," said Skinny.

"Who is your best friend?"
  asked Fats.

"Don't you remember?"
asked Skinny.

"No," said Fats.

"I will give you a clue," said Skinny.

"He is fun."

"That is good," said Fats.

"I think so, too," said Skinny.

"Do you remember now?"

Fats tapped his head.

Tap, tap, tap.

"No," he said.

"Give me more clues."

"Okay," said Skinny.
"I will give you three more clues.
I will write them down."

CLUE #1 My best friend is fun.

CLUE #2 My best friend is nice.

CLUE #3 My best friend is very,
very fat.

CLUE #4 Today my best friend
is wearing purple overalls.

Fats read the clues.

He tapped his head.

Tap, tap, tap.

"I am fun," he said.

"I know," said Skinny.

"I am nice," said Fats.

Skinny nodded. "I know that, too."

"I am very, very fat," Fats said.

Fats looked down.

"And today,
I am wearing purple overalls!"
Fats smiled so hard his eyes closed.
"I must be your best friend!" he said.
"Yes," said Skinny.
"You are my best friend."

Chapter Two
Going to Mars

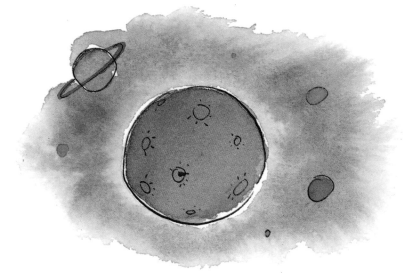

"Let's go to Mars," said Fats.

"How do we do that?"
  asked Skinny.

"We need a rocket," said Fats.

"We can build one tomorrow."

The next day Skinny asked,

"How do we build a rocket?"

Fats tapped his head.

Tap, tap, tap.

"We need a seat.

We need an alarm clock.

We need a very, very large spring."

"Is that all?

Are you sure?" asked Skinny.

"I am sure!" said Fats.

Soon the two friends
were building the rocket.
It was not going well.
The seat was not big enough.
"Move over, Skinny!"
Brrrinnnnggg!
Brrrinnnnggg!
The alarm clock would
not stop ringing.

And the spring flung them
into a tree.
It did not fling them to Mars.
"WHOOOA!"

"I give up!" said Fats.

He stomped his hooves so hard,
he got stuck in the mud.

He started to cry.

"I am not good at anything!"

"Yes, you are," said Skinny.

He pulled Fats out of the mud.

"I am?" asked Fats.

"You are good at getting
stuck in the mud," said Skinny.

"Very funny," said Fats.

"What else?"

"You are good at making
Marshmallow Pie."
Fats smiled. "That is true.
What else?"

"You are good at being
   a best friend," said Skinny.
"Oh, Skinny!" said Fats.
   He threw his arm
   around his friend.
"Let's go have some
   Marshmallow Pie."

Chapter Three
Marshmallow Pie

Fats opened the cupboard.

"Oh dear," he said.

"I am out of Marshmallow Pie."

"We can make one. What do
we need?" said Skinny.

Fats tapped his head.

Tap, tap, tap.

"We need chocolate cookies.

We need marshmallows.

We need *lots* and *lots*

of chocolate sauce."

"I will go to the store," said Skinny.

Soon Skinny was back.

Fats looked in the bag.

"This is not chocolate sauce!

These are not chocolate cookies!"

he said.

"I got carrot cookies
and carrot sauce instead,"
said Skinny.
"I think it will be good."
"I think it will be yucky!" said Fats.
"I do not want any!"
Skinny shrugged.
He made the pie all by himself.
First he stomped on the carrot cookies.
Stomp! Stomp! Stomp!
Then Skinny swept up the crumbs.
He sang:
"La, la, la. I love to make pie!
I crush the crumbs.
I sweep the crumbs.
I put them in the dish.

I pour in the marshmallows.

I pour on the sauce.

More sauce. More sauce,

more sauce, sauce."

"There!" said Skinny.

"Doesn't it look good?"

Fats shrugged.

It did look good.

But he did not want to say so.

"Too bad you do not want any,"

said Skinny.

Skinny took the first bite.

"Mmmmmm!"

"Is it good?" asked Fats.

"Mmmmmm-mmmmmm!" said Skinny.

"Is it better than my chocolate
   Marshmallow Pie?"
   asked Fats.

"Mmmmmm-mmmmmm-mmmmmm!"
   said Skinny.

Fats started to drool.

"Can I have a teensy-weensy bite?"
he asked.

Skinny did what all best friends
would do.

He gave Fats the rest of the pie.
"Mmmmmm-mmmmmm-
mmmmmm-mmmmmm!"

Make Fats's Marshmallow Pie!

YOU WILL NEED:

1 package of chocolate graham crackers

1 package of large marshmallows

1 jar of chocolate sauce

STEPS:

1. Crush the graham crackers. But

   don't use your feet like Skinny!

2. Put the crushed crackers in a pie dish.

3. Spread the marshmallows over

   the crackers.

4. Pour on the jar of chocolate sauce.

5. Eat!

Like Skinny, you can make up your own flavors

of Marshmallow Pie! Try making a Marshmallow

Pie with strawberry or caramel sauce. . . .

Mmmmmm-mmmmmm-mmmmmm!